SHADOW
SQUADRON

PHANTOM
SUN

ZO13.671

SHADOW
SQUADRON

PHANTOM SUN

WRITTEN BY
CARL BOWEN

ILLUSTRATED BY
WILSON TORTOSA

AND
BENNY FUENTES

2012.Z41

AUTHORIZING

Raintree is an imprint of Capstone Global Library
Limited, a company incorporated in England and
Wales having its registered office at 7 Pilgrim
Street, London, EC4V 6LB   Registered company
number: 6695582

www.raintreepublishers.co.uk
myorders@raintreepublishers.co.uk

First published by Stone Arch Books © 2014
First published in the United Kingdom in 2014

The moral rights of the proprietor have been
asserted.

Designed by Brann Garvey

ISBN 978 1 406 27562 9 (paperback)
17 16 15 14 13
10 9 8 7 6 5 4 3 2 1

British Library Cataloguing in Publication Data
A full catalogue record for this book is available
from the British Library

Printed in China.

CONTENTS

(316.981)

SHADOW SQUADRON DOSSIER

CROSS, RYAN

RANK: Lieutenant Commander
BRANCH: Navy Seal
PSYCH PROFILE: Cross is the team leader of Shadow Squadron. Control oriented and loyal, Cross insisted on hand-picking each member of his squad.

WALKER, ALONSO

RANK: Chief Petty Officer
BRANCH: Navy Seal
PSYCH PROFILE: Walker is Shadow Squadron's second-in-command. His combat experience, skepticism, and distrustful nature make him a good counter-balance to Cross's leadership.

YAMASHITA, KIMIYO

RANK: Lieutenant
BRANCH: Army Ranger
PSYCH PROFILE: The team's sniper is an expert marksman and a true stoic. It seems his emotions are as steady as his trigger finger.

BRIGHTON, EDGAR

RANK: Staff Sergeant
BRANCH: Air Force Combat Controller
PSYCH PROFILE: The team's technician and close-quarters-combat specialist is popular with his squadmates but often agitates his commanding officers.

PHOTO NOT AVAILABLE

JANNATI, ARAM

RANK: Second Lieutenant
BRANCH: Army Ranger
PSYCH PROFILE: Jannati serves as the team's linguist. His sharp eyes serve him well as a spotter, and he's usually paired with Yamashita on overwatch.

PHOTO NOT AVAILABLE

SHEPHERD, MARK

RANK: Lieutenant
BRANCH: Army (Green Beret)
PSYCH PROFILE: The heavy-weapons expert of the group, Shepherd's love of combat borders on unhealthy.

2019.681

OPERATION

PHANTOM SUN 5678

An unknown aircraft has crashed in Antarctica near a remote science facility. Shadow Squadron has been tasked with recovering the device. Early reports show that Russian Special Forces are already on the scene, meaning we need to keep a low profile and avoid hostilities if at all possible.

Upon landing, we'll rendezvous with a psy-ops spook from Phantom Cell who has more information on the situation. I don't need to remind you, gentlemen, that stealth is of paramount importance for this mission.

3245.98 ● ● ●

— Lieutenant Commander Ryan Cross

PRIMARY OBJECTIVE(S)

- Locate & secure crashed aircraft

- Maintain anonymity

SECONDARY OBJECTIVE(S)

- Avoid hostilities with Russian
  Special Forces

1932.789

0412.981

1624.054

INTEL

DECRYPTING

12345

COM CHATTER

- INTEL: intelligence, or information relevant to a mission
- JSOC: Joint Special Operations Command, or Command for short
- PSY-OPS: psychological operations
- PT: physical training
- SONIC BOOM: a loud noise made when passing the speed of sound

3245.98

CHAPTER ONE

SONIC BOOM

Lieutenant Commander Ryan Cross was already in the briefing room when the rest of his team arrived. Shadow Squadron had been carefully pieced together from elite soldiers of the special operations forces of the various US military branches. Represented among them were Navy SEALs, Green Berets, Army Rangers, an Air Force Combat Controller, a Navy corpsman, and a Marine Force Recon specialist.

In short, Shadow Squadron was the top special operations team, and the average citizen knew absolutely nothing about them. Shadow Squadron was tasked with secretly protecting America's interests and defending its people through top-secret, black operations all over the world. They took action where the regular forces would not or could not go.

Lieutenant Commander Cross was proud and honoured to serve as the squad's commanding officer. At the moment, however, the seven men under his direct command didn't give the impression that they shared his honour and pride in their work. In fact, they didn't look much like the squad of highly trained professionals that he knew they were. Right now, more than anything, they looked tired. It was just after 0500 hours local time, and none of them shared his enthusiasm for the dawn's early light.

The men filed in quietly with heavy eyes and slow footsteps, many of them clutching mugs of steaming coffee. Each of them carried English muffin sandwiches stuffed full of scrambled eggs, bacon, ham, cheese, and whatever else they could shovel in.

"All right, you herd of turtles," the last man grumbled as he came into the room. "Shuffle in and sit down."

The speaker was Chief Petty Officer Alonso Walker, Cross's second-in-command. Like Cross, Walker had come to Shadow Squadron from the Navy SEALs, though his training had been more focused and specialized than Cross's. Walker had been with the team since the creation of the programme. In the beginning, Walker had resented Cross's authority. Recently, however, Walker had grown to like Cross – and showed him respect on and off the battlefield.

Walker demonstrated that respect by coming into the briefing room balancing an extra breakfast sandwich on top of his own and precariously clinging to the handle of a second mug of coffee in his other hand. The Chief set the extra sandwich and coffee down in front of Cross, then took his position at the other corner.

"Thanks, Chief," Cross said. "You didn't have to do that." Cross neglected to add the reason why:

he'd already eaten breakfast an hour ago.

"No problem," Walker grumbled, barely audible, as he hunched over his coffee, avoiding eye contact with everyone. "So is there a reason we're having this briefing before we've even done PT?"

"Yep," Cross replied. He took a sip of coffee for the sake of politeness – it was pitch black, the way Walker liked it.

Cross tapped the touchscreen on the surface of the table. A section of the wall slid open to reveal a high-definition LED screen. It showed the swords-and-globe emblem of the Joint Special Operations Command. Another tap and swipe brought up a still image of two men wearing heavy, red snow parkas as they rode away on a snowmobile. The camera peered over the shoulder of another parka-clad individual on a second snowmobile. Both vehicles made their way across a desolate, white expanse of snow and ice under a grey sky.

At the sight of the image, Staff Sergeant Edgar Brighton gasped in excitement and immediately sucked a mouthful of his breakfast down the wrong pipe. He pointed at the screen, his eyes watering, as he coughed and choked.

"Medic," Cross said dryly.

"I just saw this!" Brighton finally managed to say. "It's real? Are we dealing with this?"

"Why is Brighton freaking out?" Walker asked.

"It's real," Cross replied to Brighton first. He addressed his next word to Walker and the others. "Watch."

At that, Cross tapped his touchscreen to start the video. The thrum of the snowmobiles' engines and the whistling of hard wind burst from the speakers in the briefing room. Cross tapped the touchscreen once more to mute the video.

"You're not missing anything without sound," he explained as the men in red rode through the snow. The camera bobbed and bounced with the motion of the snowmobile in the hands of the person carrying it. "These guys are geologists from Lost Aspen, an American mobile research station in Marie Byrd Land, in western Antarctica. What

they're up to here isn't relevant to our mission."
He checked the screen and waited for a visual cue,
then said, "But this is."

"And it's flippin' awesome!" Brighton added.

On the screen, the geologists started pointing
and waving frantically. The lead snowmobile's
passenger shook the shoulders of the driver, who
then brought the snowmobile to a halt. The
cameraman's driver stopped alongside them. More
frantic gesturing from the first geologist made the
rest look up to see what he was pointing at. The
camera watched them for a few more seconds,
then lurched around in a half circle and tilted up
at the sky. Clouds wavered in and out of focus for
a second before the cameraman found what the
others had pointed at – a lance of white fire in the
sky. The image focused, showing what appeared
to be a meteorite, with a trailing white plume,
punching through a hole in the clouds. The camera
zoomed out to allow the cameraman to better track
the meteorite's progress through the sky.

"Is that a meteorite?" Shepherd asked.

"Just keep watching," Brighton said, breathless with anticipation.

Right on cue, the supposed meteorite suddenly flared white, then changed directions in mid-flight by almost 45 degrees. Grunts and hisses of surprise filled the room.

"So ... not a meteorite," Shepherd muttered.

The members of Shadow Squadron watched in awe as the falling object changed direction once again, with another flare, and pitched downwards. The camera angle twisted overhead and then lowered to track its Earth-ward trajectory.

"And now ... sonic boom," Brighton said.

The camera image shook violently as the compression wave from the falling object broke the speed of sound and the accompanying burst shook the cameraman's hands. A moment later, the object streaked into the distance and disappeared into the rolling hills of ice and snow. The video footage ended a few moments later with a still image of the gawking geologists looking like a bunch of kids on Christmas morning.

"This video popped up on the internet a few hours ago," Cross said. "It's already starting to go viral."

"What is it?" Second Lieutenant Aram Jannati said. Jannati, the team's newest member, came from the Marine Special Operations Regiment. "I can't imagine we'd get involved in this if it was just a meteor."

"Meteorite," Staff Sergeant Adam Paxton said. "If it gets through the atmosphere to the ground, it's a meteorite, not a meteor."

Brighton hopped out of his chair. "That wasn't a meteorite, man," he said. He dug his smartphone out of his pocket and came round the table to the front of the room. He laid his phone on the touchscreen Cross had, then synced up the two devices. With that done, Brighton used his phone as a remote control to run the video back to the first time the object had changed directions. He used a slider to move the timer back and forth, repeatedly showing the object's sharp angle of deflection through the sky.

"Meteorites can't change directions like this," Brighton said. "This is 45 degrees of deflection at least, and the thing barely even slows down. And it did it *twice*."

"I'm seeing a flare when it turns," Paxton said. "Meteors hold a lot of frozen water when they're in space, and it expands when it reaches the atmosphere. If those gases vented or exploded, couldn't that cause a change in direction?"

"Not this sharply," Brighton said before Cross could reply. "Besides, if you look at this..." He used a few swipes across his phone to pause the video and zoom in on the flying object. At the new resolution, a dark oblong shape was visible inside a wreath of fire. He then advanced through the first and second changes of direction and tracked it a few seconds forward before pausing again. "See?"

A room full of shrugs and uncomprehending looks met Brighton's eager gaze.

Brighton tossed his hands up in mock frustration. "It's the same size!" he said. "If this thing had exploded twice – with enough force to push something this big in a different direction both times – it would be in a million pieces. So those aren't explosions. They're thrusters or ramjets or something."

"Which makes this what?" Shepherd asked. "A UFO?"

"Sure," Paxton answered in a mocking tone. "It's unidentified, it's flying, and it's surely an object."

"You don't know that it's not a UFO," Brighton said. "I mean, this thing could very well be from outer space!"

"Sit down, Sergeant," Chief Walker said.

Brighton reluctantly did so and pocketed his phone.

"Don't get ahead of yourself, Ed," Cross added, taking back control of the briefing. "Phantom Cell analysts have authenticated the video and concluded that this thing is some kind of metal construct, though they can't make out specifics from the quality of the video. I suppose it's possible it's from outer space, but it's much more likely it's man-made. The only thing we know for sure is that it's not American-made. Therefore, our mission is to get out to where it came down, zip it up, and bring it back for a full analysis. Any questions so far?"

"I have one," Jannati said. "What is Phantom Cell?"

Cross nodded. As the newest member of the team, Jannati wasn't as familiar with the JSOC's various secret programmes. "Phantom Cell is a parallel programme to ours," Cross explained. "But their focus is on psy-ops, cyberwarfare, and research and development."

Jannati nodded. "Geeks, in other words," he said. Brighton gave him a sour look but said nothing.

"What are we supposed to do about the scientists who found this thing?" Lieutenant Kimiyo Yamashita asked. True to his stoic and patient nature, the sniper had finished his breakfast and coffee while everyone else was talking excitedly. "Do they know we're coming?"

Cross frowned. "That's the problem," he said.

"We haven't heard a peep out of them since this video appeared online. Attempts at contacting them have gone unanswered. Last anyone heard, the geologists who made the video were going to try to find the point of impact where this object came down. We have no idea whether they found it or what happened to them."

"Isn't this how the movie *Aliens* started?" Brighton asked. "With a space colony suddenly cutting off communication after a UFO crash landing?"

Paxton rolled his eyes. "Lost Aspen's pretty new, and it's in the middle of Antarctica," he said. "It could just be a simple technical failure."

"You have zero imagination, man," Brighton said. "You're going to be the first one the monster eats. Well … after me, anyway." Several of the men laughed.

"These are our orders," Cross continued as if he had never been interrupted in the first place. "Locate the crashed object, bring it back for study, figure out why the research station stopped communicating, and make sure the civilians are safe. Stealth is going to be of paramount importance on this one. Nobody has any territorial claims on Marie Byrd Land, but no country is supposed to be sending troops on missions anywhere in Antarctica, either."

"Are we expecting anyone else to be breaking that rule besides us, Commander?" Yamashita asked.

"It's possible," Cross said. "If this object is man-made, whoever made it is probably going to come looking for it. And any other government that attached the same significance to the video that ours did will send people, too. No specific intel has been confirmed yet, but we've heard whispers of Russian Special Forces on the scene."

"Seems like the longer the video's out there, the more likely we're going to have company," Yamashita said.

"About that," Cross said. "Phantom Cell's running a psy-ops campaign in support of our efforts. They're simultaneously spreading the word that the video's a hoax and doing their best to stop it from spreading by eliminating circulation."

"Good luck to them on that last one," Brighton said. "You can't stop the internet. Phantom Cell's good, but nobody's *that* good."

"Not our concern," Cross said. "We ship out in one hour, so get your gear on the Commando. We'll go over more mission specifics during the flight. Understood?"

"Sir," the men responded in unison. At a nod from Cross, they rose and gathered up the remains of their breakfasts. As they left the briefing room, Walker remained behind. He gulped down the last of his coffee before standing up.

"Brighton's sure excited," Walker said.

"I knew he would be," Cross replied. "I didn't expect him to try to help out so much with the briefing, though."

Walker hesitated for a moment. "Is that what I'm like whenever I chip in from up here?" he asked.

Cross fought off the urge to toy with his second-in-command, but he couldn't stop a mischievous smile from creeping across his face. "Maybe a little bit," he said.

Walker returned Cross's grin. "Then I wholeheartedly apologize," he said.

INTEL

DECRYPTING
IIIIIIII IIIIIIIIIIIIIIIIII

12345

COM CHATTER

- AHKIO: sled used to carry things

- CAVALIER: if you are cavalier, you
  show a lack of proper concern for
  something

- SHORTS: ski-shoes used for
  traversing snow and ice

- UAV: unmanned aerial vehicle, or a
  drone

3245.98 ● ● ●

PARALLEL SUNS

After several monotonous hours of flying in the MC130-J Commando II plane, Shadow Squadron made a single stop to transfer to a CH-53E Super Stallion transport helicopter. A few hours more, and the team was finally at its destination.

The blank, unbroken expanse of Marie Byrd Land, Antarctica, stretched out below. Half of the ground was obscured by cloud cover and glare from the sun.

As Cross peered down the horizon, he saw what looked like two parallel suns. "Am I hallucinating?" he asked, pointing at the strange sight.

Brighton answered him. "No, sir," he said excitedly. "That's a phantom sun. It's a phenomenon that occurs when sunlight is refracted through ice crystals. Pretty cool, if you ask me." Brighton nudged Yamashita in the ribs. "Kinda looks like a sniper scope's reticule, huh?"

"No," Yamashita answered flatly. He shot Cross an annoyed look.

"I'm sorry I asked," Cross said with a chuckle. Brighton was usually pretty excited on missions, but he seemed to be especially enthusiastic about this one.

As the Super Stallion began its descent, Cross clapped once to get his men's attention. "I know you've all been through Pickel Meadows and Kodiak and Black Rapids," he said, referring to the Marines', Navy's, and Army's respective northern and mountain training centres. "But this isn't going to be exactly like that. For one thing, it's actually summer right now in Antarctica. Temperatures could get up to a balmy 60 out on the coast – a little colder inland where we are. For another, it's not going to get dark. At all. The sun won't set down here for another month at least. That means you won't be able to rely on it for direction, either. Also, remember what Williams said about whiteout and snow blindness – keep your sunglasses on at all times when we're outdoors."

WHUMP!

The helicopter thumped down hard onto the thickly packed Antarctic ice. Cross supervised his team's last-minute gear checks, then ordered the flight crew to lower the rear cargo hatch.

WOOOOOOSH!

Frigid wind clawed its way into the cargo bay, easily overpowering the wall-mounted space heaters. Cross couldn't help but check to make sure everyone was properly bundled in their cold-weather gear.

"Commander?" Yamashita called, drawing Cross's attention back to the cargo ramp. The sniper stood at the top, facing down and outside towards something Cross couldn't see. His voice had the same tone of guarded caution Cross heard when Yamashita was waiting for the go-ahead to take a shot with his M110 rifle.

Cross walked over to Yamashita and found him staring at a stranger standing mid-way up the ramp with his hands out at both sides. The stranger wasn't dressed in a military-issue, seven-layer Extended Cold Weather Clothing System (or ECWCS) like the members of Cross's team. Nor was he dressed like the airfield skeleton crew Cross could see coming towards the plane from further off to refuel it. This man's winter gear was all expensive, store-brand stuff that might as well have had the price tags still attached for how new it all looked.

Cross tilted his head as an introduction, wondering if the man was some civilian scientist who'd accidentally wandered into a place he shouldn't be.

"Lieutenant Commander Ryan Cross, I presume?" the stranger asked. He grinned. "Permission to come aboard, sir?"

"Who are you and what are you doing out here?" Cross demanded. The tone of the stranger's voice and the smug confidence in his grin reminded Cross of himself when he was much younger. It was an unpleasant mirror to gaze into.

"Bill Dyer," the man said. "From Phantom Cell. I've been assigned to your squadron for the duration of this mission."

"So you say," Cross replied. "How'd you get here so fast?" The men behind Cross read the tension in his body language and stopped to watch how things would play out.

Dyer's grin widened. "I was already on assignment not far from here," he said. "I hitched a ride with the ground crew."

"I'll have to confirm this with Command," Cross said.

"Sure, sure," Dyer said amiably.

Cross turned and headed back to the helicopter's cockpit, giving Yamashita a look as he turned. Yamashita nodded his understanding and remained in Cross's place to glare at Dyer.

Picking up on the hint, Dyer strolled down the ramp and stood out of the way as Shadow Squadron continued to unload gear.

A quick call back to Command confirmed Dyer's story and earned Cross an apology for the slow communication. He informed his men of the change in plans and approached Dyer once more.

"You're legit," Cross said. "Sorry about that."

"No harm done," Dyer said, as if Cross hadn't kept him waiting. "And welcome to Pluto." That joke drew a chuckle from Brighton.

Cross looked around. The outpost where they'd landed extended into a blue-ice runway that continued for miles until it disappeared from sight. There were also two drab, pre-fabricated, semi-cylindrical buildings that were partially buried in snow and ice. They looked like giant cans that'd been dropped carelessly into the ground.

"Camp's not much to look at," Dyer said, noticing Cross's skepticism. "It's been abandoned for a few years since the Pine Island Glacier camp opened up. That one's a little more central and convenient to the stations that use it. We still had this place on record, though, and thought it would serve as a nice out-of-the-way base of operations. The ground crew cleaned the place out and got it up and running. In another few weeks, it might actually be warm in the main building. I wouldn't hold my breath, though."

Cross nodded for him to continue.

"The good news is," Dyer said, "I've been able to pinpoint the crash site you're here to find. It's only a dozen or so miles away, between us and Lost Aspen. I figure we should go ahead and check out the crash site first."

"How did you find it?" Brighton asked.

"It wasn't too hard," Dyer said with a cavalier shrug. "I'm the one who caused the crash, after all."

Stunned silence followed that claim. Cross was the first to break it. "Come again?"

"Yeah, what is it?" Brighton asked.

"It's a hunter-killer drone satellite," Dyer explained. "Think of it like an orbital UAV. I caught it trying to hack into one of our spy satellites and engaged in a tug-of-war with its operator. I locked him out and stole it from him, but I couldn't keep it from crashing."

"Who built it?" Brighton asked with childlike fascination.

"Probably the Chinese," Dyer said. "Regardless, the operator was definitely Chinese. I've crossed swords with him a few times, so to speak. I was able to blind him from where the drone crashed, so we've got a head start. But it's only going to be a matter of time before they figure that internet video out and come looking, so we need to get to the site in a hurry."

"All right," Cross said, annoyed with the way the Phantom Cell operative casually gave orders as if he were in charge. "As soon as the snowmobiles are ready and we get our gear set up, we'll head out there and check it out."

Dyer winced. "Actually, Commander, I was just coming to that," he said. "Snowmobiles might not be an option right now – unless you've got some of those Canadian stealth jobs."

"Canada has stealth snowmobiles?" Walker asked, his tone doubtful.

"Yeah, they're pretty cool, Chief," Brighton said. "They're hybrid-electric with like a 150-mile range. They can get up to, like, 50 miles per hour. I think they call them..." He looked back and forth between Walker and Cross, neither of whom looked glad for his input. "Anyway, they're neat."

"Edgar Brighton," Dyer said, extending a hand. "It's a pleasure. Bill Dyer, Phantom Cell. We heard about what you did with the Avenger drone over Saraqeb. Impressive stuff."

"Thanks, man!" Brighton said, shaking Dyer's hand. If Brighton was at all disappointed to find that the object that had crashed wasn't an alien spaceship, he didn't show it. "Sounds kind of like what you did with this satellite drone thing."

Dyer winked. "Like I said, impressive."

"What's this about not using the snowmobiles?" Cross cut in.

"We'll talk later, when you've got a minute," Dyer said to Brighton. To Cross, he said, "Silence is going to be golden on this one, Commander. The Chinese might not know where to look for their drone yet, but the Russians are already on the case. They landed a team a few hours before you guys got here."

"Are they scientists?" Chief Walker asked.

"Nope," Dyer said. "My information indicates they're Spetsnaz. I think they're responsible for the communications blackout from Lost Aspen. No confirmation on that intel, though."

"Russian Special Forces," Cross said. "Could be worse, I guess. We're not technically enemies with them anymore."

"Just calling them Spetsnaz doesn't tell us much," Walker said. "You know anything more about the specific unit in play?"

Dyer shook his head. "Wish I did," he said. "But

according to radio intercepts, they're definitely Russian and definitely here because of the video. They're ahead of us, but I can't say if they've found the site or not. They cut me off before I could learn more."

"Regardless, they're out there right now," Cross said. "Watching, listening, and with no more right to be here than we have. You're correct – we can't risk a noisy approach."

"Plus," Dyer added, "if they know that you know they're here, they'll go to some lengths to make sure you don't tell anybody. You know, since none of us are supposed to be here at all."

"Possibly," Walker said.

"It's something you guys should be considering as well," Dyer said. "I mean, as soon as they know we're here, it might be wise to…"

"No," Cross said. "That isn't how we operate. If operational security becomes a problem, we'll deal with it in due time. The Russians aren't my main concern, though – the scientists are. Making sure they are safe is our top priority."

"With respect, Commander," Dyer said, "the drone is the top priority."

"That's what it says on our orders," Cross said. "But I'm in charge here, and I decide what's most important. If you don't like that, you can take it up with Command."

"Duly noted," Dyer said neutrally.

"In any event," Cross continued, "the crash site's between us and Lost Aspen. We'll stop by there to see what we can see on the way. Got it?"

"I'm just an observer and technical advisor," Dyer said with a shrug. "You guys are the ones with the weapons. We'll do it your way."

"All right then," Cross said. He turned away to address his men. They quickly gathered around to listen. "We've confirmed there's a rival team on the field: Russian Special Forces – we don't know how many. They've got a head start, but we don't know how much of one. I don't need to remind you of the sticky legal situation our being here represents. Suffice it to say, this operation just went from top-secret to full black. That means total noise discipline en route. We're leaving the snowmobiles behind and going out on the shorts. We'll recon the crash site and secure it if we're first on the scene, then radio back for the Super Stallion. I want you to finish unloading your gear, stretch your legs, change your socks, carb up, and hydrate. Then load up your ahkios because we're leaving in twenty minutes."

"Sir," the men responded.

When Cross finished, Dyer looked at him and pretended to cough behind his hand.

"Right, one more thing," Cross said. "This is Bill Dyer of Phantom Cell. He's coming with us as an advisor. He's the reason we're here, so I need a volunteer to buddy up and keep an eye on him."

"Can you ski?" Shepherd asked with a skeptical frown. "Or shoot? Did you even bring a gun?"

"Yes to all three," Dyer said. "My rifle's with the rest of my gear. And yeah, I can ski and shoot. I was an alternate on the '94 Olympic men's biathlon team."

Paxton smirked. "Didn't the Russians take home the most gold in biathlon that year?" he asked.

"Only because I didn't get to compete against them," Dyer assured him.

"Thank you for volunteering, Sergeant," Cross said to Paxton. "Make sure Dyer and his gear are ready to go when we are."

"Sir," Paxton said.

"Twenty minutes, people," Cross reiterated to the whole team. "Get started."

INTEL

DECRYPTING
IIII I IIII   III II IIII IIII IIII | IIII I

12345

COM CHATTER

- GPS: global positioning system, or an electronic system that uses satellites to determine one's position

- INFRARED: in terms of optics, infrared vision lets the viewer see heat signatures

- M110: an American-made, semi-automatic sniper rifle

3245.98 ● ● ●

CHAPTER THREE

OPTICS

The first leg of Shadow Squadron's journey to the crash site proceeded without incident. The team set out on their shorts, which combined the best features of skis and snowshoes. The carbon fibre ski-shoes offered a wide, flat base for moving over loose powder or uphill. They also had a set of corrugated scales beneath the soles of the soldiers' boots which offered traction without inhibiting forward motion.

Dyer was geared similarly, but once again his equipment was top-of-the-line professional sports gear rather than the field-tested special order equipment Shadow Squadron soldiers used.

As they travelled, the soldiers wore their seven-layer ECWCS outfits with digital white-blue-grey camouflage. They carried their rifles on their backs. The rest of their gear they dragged behind them in lightweight carbon fibre ahkio sleds attached to harnesses on their belts. The only exception in this case was Dyer, who had only brought a heavy backpack and had no sleds.

The sun and its double looped through the sky, flirting with the horizon but never quite touching it. Cross resisted the urge to go all the way to the crash site immediately. He was concerned that the lack of a regular day-and-night cycle would cause him to accidentally push his men too hard and wear them out early. When his compass and GPS told him the team was still a couple of miles from the crash site, he ordered them to stop and make camp.

The men dug down several feet through the ice and snow and set up tents along with an electric field stove. Then the team ate and took turns resting for the long trip to follow.

Although Dyer had stayed by Paxton's side

for the whole trip thus far, Cross noticed that the Phantom Cell operative had barely said a word to the Green Beret once camp was set up. Instead, Dyer spent most of his time talking to Brighton, praising the short-range Four-Eyes UAV drone that Brighton had designed. Then he went on to engage him in a discussion of computing and surveillance technology that sounded more like science fiction speculation to Cross than anything with real-world applications. Then again, Cross hadn't been able to imagine anything like smartphones or UAV drones when he'd first joined the Navy, but those things were everywhere now.

Since the pair of them were getting along so well, Cross reassigned Brighton to keep an eye on Dyer, which suited both men just fine. Paxton privately admitted to being relieved as well after Cross informed him of the switch. Paxton couldn't explain exactly why, but something about Dyer rubbed him the wrong way. Cross didn't respond to Paxton's concern, but his impression of Dyer was much the same. The man had an air of competence and charisma about him, but it was an oily sort of charisma. A youthful kind of cockiness that flew in the face of caution for the sake of success.

"That could be it," Chief Walker said after Cross expressed his concerns. "Or it could be you're just getting old, Commander. Same stuff comes to mind when I think about you most days." Walker tried to hide his smirk behind his tin coffee cup.

"I see," Cross said. "Thanks for that, Chief."

"Anytime, sir."

Some hours later, the soldiers broke camp and set out in silence once again. They made remarkable time, moving primarily downhill over smooth terrain. Well before lunchtime, they topped a small hill, which gave them their first view of the site where the drone had crashed.

Cross called everyone to a stop. The men gathered up around him. "This is the place," he said. "And it's right where you said it would be, Dyer. Good work."

"Maths," Dyer replied with a shrug of humility. Cross didn't buy it.

The site itself wasn't all that impressive. The impact crater was comet-shaped where the drone had come in at a shallow angle. It had melted a trail and gouged a hole in the frozen landscape. Cottony diamond dust settled low over the area, making the air sparkle.

"Binoculars," Cross said. "Glass and FLIR. Let's take a look around before we get down there."

The soldiers drew their ahkios in close and kneeled over their ski-shoes to examine the crash site with field binoculars and forward-looking infrared (or FLIR) binoculars. Dyer got down beside Brighton and scanned the area with a single-lens FLIR spyglass.

Yamashita kicked out of his ski-shoes to lie prone at the crest of the hill. He lay looking casually over the area with the Leupold scope on his M110 sniper rifle. A taut mesh of loose-weave white nylon covered the end of his scope, though it didn't seem to obscure his vision. "No wreckage," Yamashita said.

"No scientists, either," Walker added, peering

through one of the sets of FLIR binoculars. "Or Russians."

"I see tracks," Cross said. "Snowmobile tracks back and forth on the far side. The ones leading out have a heavy trench behind and between them. They don't look that fresh. Probably from the geologists. There are ski tracks too that come in from a different angle. Looks like they head off in the direction the snowmobiles came from. They're fresher, too."

"They're probably from the Russians," Walker said. "Tracking the geologists."

"*Hunting* them," Dyer corrected.

"If my read's right," Cross said, "the scientists in the video found this site, attached the drone to their snowmobiles, and then dragged it back to Lost Aspen. Sometime later, the Russians showed up and followed the trail back. They could be at Lost Aspen already."

"They almost certainly are," Dyer said. "It's time to consider a full –"

Cross was about to set Dyer straight on who was giving the orders when the ground several feet down the hill in front of them suddenly sprayed a double-handful of snow in the air.

FOOSH!

Cross flinched and watched the tiny white flakes drift back to earth.

"What the heck?" Dyer asked, looking just as surprised as Cross felt.

FOOSH!!

Another puff of snow shot up in front of Walker's feet. "Sniper!" Yamashita hissed, figuring it out at the same time Cross did. "Sniper – find cover!"

Cross and Walker dived away, hoping to put the crest of their small hill between themselves and the shooter. Brighton, meanwhile, lurched out of his ski-shoes to tackle Dyer to the ground.

CRACK!!!

A sharp noise broke the eerie silence of the attack. Both Brighton and Dyer yelped in surprise and pain as they landed in a tangle of arms and legs and rolled down the hill, bumping awkwardly over Dyer's bulky backpack. Williams, the team's medic, popped out of his ski-shoes and crawl-slid over to them to check for injuries.

"Sleds up!" Cross ordered, yanking his ahkio up beside him where he lay, hauling it one-handed to the hilltop.

The others began to do the same, balancing their sleds on their edges in the snow, using the weight of the gear strapped on top of the sleds to keep them balanced upright. They lined up the ahkios in a crooked line that looked like the tops of a medieval castle wall, then they hunkered down behind them. The advanced carbon fibre skin over the lightweight metal core of the sleds made them somewhat bullet resistant, if not bulletproof. In any case, the sleds offered better cover than the snowy nothingness all around them.

With the quick-and-dirty wall erected, Cross motioned for the others to move back down the hill away from it and slide over to the left. While he'd seen video of the sleds stopping small-arms fire, he didn't want to test his luck against a high-powered sniper rifle. He also didn't want the sniper to get lucky by arcing his shots over the makeshift wall. When the others were relocated, only Yamashita remained on the line, lying exactly where he'd been the whole time. He hadn't flinched at the signs of gunfire, nor had he moved his sled into line with the others. He just lay perfectly still, looking downrange through his Leupold scope with the patience of a stone.

Cross came to check on Brighton and Dyer. "They're all right, Commander," Williams said. "No blood, no foul. Neither one of them was hit."

"Jerk blew up my binoculars," Brighton said. He sat up and showed Cross the remains of the black-and-grey FLIR lenses. They had been dangling around his neck from a long nylon lanyard when he'd tackled the Phantom Cell operative to pull him to safety. The binoculars now had a small hole on one side where the bullet had gone in and an enormous blossom of twisted metal and plastic on the other side where the bullet had exited.

"I swear to you, he will pay for that," Dyer said with all the gravity of a Shakespearean actor. "He. Will. Pay."

Brighton snickered and punched Dyer in the shoulder.

"Stay down," Cross told the two of them. To Williams he said, "Which of the sleds is yours?"

"Far left," Williams said, nodding at the sled closest to Yamashita. "Why?"

"Could be important," Cross said. "I just hope it isn't."

Without further explanation, Cross crawled back up the hill to the ahkio wall and opened Williams' gear. He dug out a medical bag and slid it back down the hill to where the medic lay waiting. Next, he picked up a pair of FLIR binoculars and edged over to the first gap in the sled wall, hoping to determine where the enemy sniper was hiding.

"Don't," Yamashita said calmly. "He'll see the glare."

He has a point, Cross realized. The sun was behind the opposing sniper, shining in Cross's eyes. In fact, it was so bitterly cold and clear that phantom suns shone to the right and left of the actual sun, giving the entire bleak landscape the look of an alien planet. Thanks to Brighton's excited explanation earlier, Cross now knew that the phantom suns were just optical illusions created by ice crystals. But that fact didn't make the sight seem any less creepy under the circumstances.

Regardless, the light was more than bright enough to cast a glare off the lenses of his binoculars and give his position away. Fortunately, the nylon mesh over the end of Yamashita's rifle scope prevented that from happening to him.

"Do you see him?" Cross whispered to Yamashita.

"I haven't fired yet, sir," Yamashita replied. "I've got eyes on a couple of likely spots, but he hasn't obliged me by moving or shooting again."

"Think we can slip behind where you think he is?" Cross asked.

"Not if he's any good," Yamashita said.

"If he were any good, he would have hit at least one of us with those first three shots," Cross argued.

"That wasn't for lack of skill," Yamashita said. "It's a problem with optics in terrain like this. Things in the distance look bigger and closer than they really are since everything is one colour. It just took him a couple of shots to adjust for difference. The fact he didn't get a kill on his third shot was pure dumb luck."

"I see," Cross said, unsettled by how close Brighton and Dyer both had apparently come to death. "This is your game. What's our next move?"

"If you can get him to shoot again without getting yourself killed, I'll take it from there, Commander," Yamashita said. He paused for a second and then added, "Well, either way … when he shoots, I can take him out."

"My soul will rest easy knowing that," Cross murmured. "Okay, hang tight. I've got an idea."

Moving carefully and hoping not to draw the enemy sniper's attention, Cross picked up the binoculars he'd been about to use. Then he rolled as fast as he could across the first gap in the sled wall to where the next two sleds sat end to end. His heart raced, fearing that the sniper would see the sudden motion and put a one-in-a-million shot through the gap. When no shot came, his heart kept racing, anyway. Cross also feared that the sniper saw the roll but was just patiently lining up a kill shot that would punch through the shield wall and into him. After another few eternally long, pulse-pounding seconds, Cross's fears dimmed to nearly nothing.

Pulling his fur-lined cap off from beneath his jacket's hood, Cross laid it down on top of the binoculars he'd grabbed. These he laid on the curved underside of one of the ski-shoes Paxton had kicked off when the warning had gone out.

Then, lying on his back behind the first of the two adjacent sleds, he used the ski-shoe to lift the hat and binoculars ever-so-slowly up over the top edge of the second sled. When it was just high enough, he propped it up on the side of the sled. His hope was that the lenses of the binoculars would cast a glare and attract the enemy sniper's attention, and that the silhouette of the hat and binoculars would look like a soldier peering up over the top of the wall –

CRACK!!!

At first, Cross didn't realize what had happened. One second he was looking up at his decoy and wondering how long it would take for the sniper to take the bait. A split-second later, the binoculars exploded as a bullet punched right through them. The hat went flying and a piece of the binoculars snapped off and flew past Cross's face, nicking his cheek.

At what seemed like the same instant, a muted cough came from Yamashita's rifle.

CRUCK.

Less than a second later, the sickening sound of impact came back from the opposite end of the crash site.

"Clear," Yamashita said. His voice was quiet and subdued, but he didn't whisper.

Cross pressed a hand to his cheek. His mitten came away with a thin, short line of blood from where the bit of shrapnel had cut him. "You sure you got him?"

Yamashita gave a small shudder that only Cross was close enough to see. "I have eyes on the target now, Commander," he said. "I got him." He said the last three words so quietly they almost disappeared in the icy wind.

"Does he have a spotter?" Cross asked. He knew Yamashita well enough by now to know not to thank him or praise the quality of his shooting.

"No," Yamashita replied.

"Must have been a sentry," Cross speculated. "Probably radioed in as soon as he saw us."

"I would have," Yamashita agreed.

Cross frowned. "That means either reinforcements are coming, or they're going to be holed up waiting for us when we get to Lost Aspen."

"Either way, we don't have much time to wait around, sir," Yamashita said.

Cross nodded. "Gear up and get your shorts back on. Take your partner and head up the path. Scout the way and find out what you can. We'll join you shortly."

"Sir," Yamashita said. He waved downhill to get Jannati's attention and signalled the Marine to join him. They paired up and Yamashita explained Cross's orders. Jannati nodded and got his gear together.

Cross descended the hill to address the remaining men. "Sniper's down," he began, "but it's more than likely the enemy knows we're here and realizes we're on the way. They're either going to meet us halfway or dig in and let us come to them."

"And they're probably going to start executing the civilians," Dyer said under his breath. "So there are no witnesses."

"You'll speak when I ask for your opinion," Cross snapped at him.

Dyer flinched. "Sir, yessir," he drawled. His tone was low and flippant, but he broke eye contact under the force of Cross's unwavering glare.

"Gear up," Cross said to his men. "We're moving out."

INTEL

DECRYPTING
||||| ||| ||||| |||| |||| |||

12345

COM CHATTER

- BALACLAVA: mask that covers the entire head and face except for the eyes and nose (and sometimes the mouth)

- AN-94: a Russian-made assault rifle

- VSS VINTOREZ: a Russian-made, quiet sniper rifle

3245.98 ● ● ●

COMRADE

To give Yamashita and Jannati time to move ahead and scout, Cross led his men over to the dead Russian sniper for a quick examination. What was left of him wasn't very helpful. The man carried no ID papers or personal mementos. The only equipment he had was a pack of energy bars, a two-way earpiece radio, a VSS Vintorez sniper rifle, and half a dozen magazines for it.

Only Cross had the stomach to remove the sniper's earpiece and dig the radio out of his coat. He looped the earpiece over his ear, opposite the one in which his own canalphone nestled. A double-pop of static indicated a signal from the sniper's comrades. Cross repeated the signal with taps on the transmitting part of the earpiece. One more pop came over the line, then a wary Russian voice spoke a single phrase.

Without pressing the earpiece to transmit, Cross looked at Walker. "Sub-shot?" he asked, repeating the Russian he'd heard as best he could repeat it. "What's that mean, Chief? Or it might have been sub-shet..."

"Report," Walker replied.

When Cross didn't answer, the voice spoke again.

"Sh-toe shloo-chee-less?" Cross relayed. "K-toe ah-nee?"

"'What happened?' maybe," Walker said. "Then, 'Who are they?' Sir, if you want me to try to talk to –"

"I've got it," Cross said.

After a long pause, Cross still did not reply. In response, the radio clicked one more time and then

fell silent. Cross cocked an eyebrow in thought, feeling every eye on him. He looked at Walker, then at Dyer before he spoke.

"How many people are stationed at Lost Aspen?" he asked.

"Forty-one," Dyer said. "Assuming your Spetsnaz counterparts haven't –"

Cross cut Dyer off with a hard glare. Then he tapped the dead Russian's radio earpiece, opening the channel.

"I know you can hear me," Cross said softly into the radio. "You and I need to talk. Sooner rather than later."

"What are you doing?" Dyer hissed. His eyes widened so much that his eyebrows completely cleared the tops of his too-expensive mirrored shades.

"Sir…" Walker said.

"Kto eto?" a flat voice said from the other end of the Russian radio frequency. It wasn't the same one that had spoken before.

"I'm going to assume," Cross said, "that you just asked me either who I am or what I want. Is that right?"

"Da," the Russian replied. Then under a heavy accent, "Yes – the first. Who are you?"

"Does it matter?" Cross asked.

"Nyet. Not really."

"So ask me what you really want to know."

"My soldier," the Russian said. "You have him?"

"No," Cross said. "He fired on us. He's dead."

The Russian made no reply for almost a minute. Cross desperately hoped the man was simply composing himself rather than ordering his men to start executing scientists. When he finally spoke again, his voice was as flat and emotionless as before. "You have any casualties?"

"No," Cross said.

"How many men are with you?" he asked.

Cross smirked. "Enough to get the job done. You?"

"More than plenty," the Russian said. "Though now one less."

"Let me bring you his remains," Cross said, causing Walker and Dyer to flinch in surprise. "This is no fit place for a soldier to rest."

"That's … an unexpected offer," the voice said. "You would do this?"

"Yes," Cross said. "In exchange for a chance to talk."

"And what have we to talk about?" he asked.

"I'd say we have 41 things left yet to talk about," Cross said. "Or 42, if you count the real reason we were both sent here."

"Indeed," the Russian said. "Very well. Bring the body to the end of the trail. We will speak there, you and I. Only you and I."

"Understood," Cross said. "Out."

He tapped the Russian earpiece one last time and removed it from his ear. Before Walker or Dyer could start in on him, Cross double-tapped his own canalphone.

"Commander?" Yamashita replied, his voice barely above a whisper.

"I take it you're in position," Cross said. "You have eyes on Lost Aspen?"

"Sir."

"Any sign of the scientists?"

"Not unless they use AN-94s in their research," Yamashita said. "If they do, then I count nine 'scientists'. Four on top of the station, two at the main door of the flag-section – that'll make sense when you see this place – and three standing guard over something wrapped up tight in white tarps. Probably the drone. Orders, sir?"

"Hang tight and don't give yourselves away," Cross said. "We're going to move up in a few minutes, then I'm going down to Lost Aspen alone to have a chat."

"Sir," Yamashita replied.

Cross turned to address the rest of Shadow Squadron as they gathered around him. "All right, here's what I want you all to do..."

It took Cross only a few minutes to unload his
ahkio then wrap and place the dead Russian sniper
on it. But in that time, he got an earful from both
Walker and Dyer about his plan. Walker was at
least respectful enough to keep his opinion pitched
low so the rest of the men didn't hear, but Dyer
objected loudly and repeatedly. Neither of them
could see what Cross hoped to gain by going into
the lion's den alone, even if the rest of the team
was watching in silence from nearby. While Cross
respected Walker's opinion, it didn't help the Chief's
case that Dyer agreed with him.

But Cross was determined to take this route. So,
once the rest of the team had moved up without
him, Cross came sliding up to Lost Aspen all alone,
pulling a corpse on a sled behind him.

Cross noticed that Lost Aspen itself was
gorgeous. Based on a group of British architects'
genius design plans, the facility resembled an
enormous metal centipede on skis. It consisted of
seven house-sized modules rising over 20 feet off the

snow on sets of four hydraulic struts functioning as broad-flat skis. Each module connected to the one behind by way of a flexible, accordion-like corridor. Six of the modules were painted glossy green. The centre module was the largest of the seven, and it had been painted in a wrap-around American flag so that the blue star-field spilled over the top and the red and white stripes wrapped around the underside. Cross had read about the British Halley VI Antarctic Research Station on which the design of Lost Aspen had been modelled. If the designs were as similar as they looked, that meant the flag section was the communal and entertainment centre for the facility.

Two guards stood posted by the main door of the flag section, just as Yamashita had reported. A quick glance around revealed seven more sentinels more or less where he had expected them. These soldiers wore layered cold-weather gear in grey-and-white camouflage print. They carried AN-94 assault rifles, and their faces were obscured by white balaclavas.

Two soldiers waited beside the tarp-wrapped

remains of the downed orbital drone. Cross spared it a glance before turning his attention to the lone figure who approached him across the ice on cleated boots.

"Here we go," Cross murmured, barely moving his lips. The comm channel remained open through the canalphone in his ear.

The Russian stopped ten feet from Cross and looked him over, his rifle in his hands but aimed at nothing. Unlike the others, he had taken his balaclava off. His face was hard-set and lined. His eyes were blue-green pools, shimmering with equal parts caution and cunning. He made no effort to hide his suspicion.

"You are he?" the Russian said. It was the same one Cross had spoken to on the radio.

Cross nodded. He gestured at the ahkio behind him. "I am. And I've brought your man."

The Russian stepped forward and extended a gloved hand, keeping his other hand on his rifle. "Give me the lead," he said.

"First let's talk about what you've got under that tarp," Cross said.

"The satellite?" the Russian said. He gestured at the science facility behind him. "Perhaps you want to talk about what's wrapped inside that garish flag first."

Cross caught his meaning and nodded. "Yes, the scientists," he said. "They're American citizens."

"As are you, I think," the Russian said. "Unless that's a Canadian accent I am hearing."

"They're civilians," Cross said. "They've got nothing to do with this. Out of all of us, they're the only ones with any right to be here."

The Russian cocked his head and peered at Cross stone-faced. "Ask me what you really want to know."

"Are they dead?" Cross asked flatly.

"No."

Cross was barely able to conceal his surprise. "No? Then what are your intentions for them?"

"I was prepared to live and let live," the Russian replied. "They need never have known we were here."

This time, Cross couldn't hide his surprise. "Come again?" he asked.

"We incapacitated them with a sleeping agent administered through the ventilation system," the Russian said.

"Like in the Dubrovka theatre?" Cross asked, his blood running cold. Spetsnaz soldiers had used a similar tactic some years ago to subdue terrorists who'd taken a theatre-full of civilians hostage in Moscow. While the terrorists had been defeated once the gas took effect, more than 100 hostages died from adverse reactions to that gas.

"That was the work of thugs," the Russian said, scowling. "No finesse. Besides, that was a decade ago." He took a deep breath, and his face returned to its neutral expression. "No, right now, the biggest risk to these people's safety is you and your men."

"How do you figure?" Cross asked.

"It is my understanding that your military does not negotiate over hostages in situations such as this," he said. "Especially not on your illegal 'black ops', yes?"

"That's not my policy," Cross said. "Personally I don't care what's under that tarp. I want to know my people are all right. I'll do whatever it takes to make sure of it."

The Russian blinked in surprise. "You are not here for the satellite, then?" he said.

"It's a secondary objective," Cross said. "Frankly, if what you're saying is true, you can walk away with it right now."

"Then I assure you it is true," the Russian said. His words rolled out slowly, as if his mind couldn't process what Cross said. "You have my word."

Cross smirked. "Give me some credit for common sense. What's that old saying? 'Trust but verify'."

The Russian cracked a smile. "As you wish. If you will come with me..."

"I'll just wait here, thanks," Cross said. He turned his head to the side and said, "All right, Sergeant. Four Eyes is a 'go'. Check things out in the middle section of the facility."

Cross turned his attention back to the Russian. "Tell your men to leave the door open," he said.

At Cross's order, Brighton remotely activated the Four Eyes UAV quad-copter that had sat unnoticed on the ahkio sled between the dead sniper's boots. The UAV hummed to life and rose to shoulder height behind Cross.

"Sir," Brighton said over Cross's canalphone.

"*Krúto*," the Russian murmured with an impressed look on his face.

"It's just a camera platform," Cross said as the UAV buzzed past him and began to slowly move towards Lost Aspen. "No weapons, no explosives."

The Russian ordered the guards at the flag module to open the doors, and one of them went inside with the UAV. Several long moments later, Brighton's voice sounded in Cross's canalphone.

"All the civilians are accounted for, sir," Brighton said. "Looks like they're all sleeping."

"Sir," Williams cut in. "They're all alive and they appear to be unconscious. I can't say more without a proper examination, but it looks like they're all right."

"Okay," Cross said, both to his men and to the Russian. "I'm satisfied."

The Russian nodded. Brighton piloted the UAV back out of the flag module and landed it next to Cross.

"All right then," Cross said. "If you and your men are willing to leave without giving us any trouble, you can take your prize and go. I'll be happy to remember we never saw you."

"And we likewise," the Russian said. His tone and expression remained wary, as if he believed he was being tricked. "Now, if I may..."

Once more, he extended a hand, palm up, reaching for the lead to the ahkio sled with his comrade's body on it. This time, Cross met him halfway and handed the lead over.

The Russian pulled the sled over to him
and knelt beside it. He grabbed a corner of the
covering Cross had used as a shroud. After a brief
hesitation, he peeled it back. The man winced at
the condition of the body that lay revealed. The
Russian's shoulders sagged for a moment, but
he was all business by the time he re-covered his
fallen comrade and stood to face Cross once again.

"We didn't expect anyone else to get here
so quickly," the Russian said, staring out at the
endless white horizon. "I only ordered him to
watch over the crash site to get him out of my hair
for a while." He sighed, and his eyes focused on
Cross's once more. "Thank you for bringing him
back."

Cross gave no reply. There was nothing he
could say that the Russian would have wanted to
hear.

"Now, we have preparations to make. Our
Mi-8 will be here within the hour. I suggest you
withdraw to wherever the rest of your men are
hiding until we are gone. I do not want to have to

explain your presence." He glanced down at the ahkio again. "I suspect I shall have more than enough to answer for."

"You and me both, comrade," Cross said.

INTEL

DECRYPTING
IIIIIIIIII IIIIIIIIIIIIIIIII

12345

COM CHATTER

- DRONE: a pilotless aircraft often controlled via remote
- CONSPIRACY THEORY: a belief based on questionable evidence that a group, like the government, is behind a secret or plot

3245.98 ● ● ●

CHAPTER FIVE

COLD LIGHT

Cross and his team regrouped at Lost Aspen. Williams, Chief Walker, and Paxton were looking after the scientists now that they'd regained consciousness. No one seemed to be suffering any ill effects from whatever chemical the Russians had used on them, but a fleet of rescue helicopters had been called in to evacuate everyone as a precaution.

In the meantime, the scientists were starting to ask questions. Dyer set to work, feeding them the simple cover story he'd made up. According to him, the US military had sent in the Marines to investigate after communication with the research

station had suddenly ceased. The soldiers had found everyone sleeping peacefully in the facility with no indication of what had happened to them. He pretended to be completely confused when they asked questions about the strange object they had recovered from the meteorite crash site. He repeated over and over that there was no evidence of any such object at the site or anywhere near Lost Aspen.

When the scientists grew more insistent, Dyer simply asked them about the object, knowing full-well that none of them could tell him anything specific since even the four scientists from the video who'd recovered it had only a vague idea of what it was. They knew it was metal and that it was man-made. Beyond that, they couldn't recall anything. And the more Dyer questioned them and worked them over, the less certain they became of the object's existence.

Cross had to admit that Dyer was good at his job. By confusing their memories of the event, he'd made their claims too insufficient for even a conspiracy theory.

After the last of the scientists were evacuated, Dyer had a brief conversation with Brighton, then left. Cross was debating the best way to ask about the discussion when Brighton approached him.

"I can't believe you just gave that device to the Russians, man," Brighton said.

"Command's not going to be happy," Cross admitted, "but I stand by my decision. I'd do it again if given the same opportunity."

"Well, sure, but what if it had been something from outer space?" Brighton asked. "I mean, baby Superman could've been in there, and now he'd Russian, thanks to you."

Cross chuckled. "That's why I keep you around, Sergeant. I value your pragmatic, grounded sense of perspective."

Although he'd expected a return laugh out of Brighton, the Combat Controller's expression clouded over. "Now that you mention it," he said, "there's something I need to talk to you about." He paused for a moment. "Dyer offered me a job."

Cross wasn't surprised. Dyer's interest in Brighton had been obvious from the start. "With Phantom Cell, I take it?" Cross asked.

"Yeah," Brighton said, staring at his boots. "Apparently part of the reason they sent him out with us was to evaluate how I operate in the field. Did you know about this?"

"First I've heard of it," Cross said. A half-smile tugged at the side of his mouth. "You didn't really have to do much this time out, though, did you?"

"I saved Dyer's life," Brighton said. "As it turns out, that goes a long way in a job interview."

Cross grew serious. "Are you going to take his offer?"

"I don't know, man," Brighton said. "Should I? I'm qualified. I can do the work – probably better than anybody I know. It's a different kind of work, though. What do you think?"

Cross considered his response carefully. "I think Phantom Cell operates very differently than we do. Remember what Dyer kept obsessing about? The drone, the drone, the drone. He didn't care about the civilians. He certainly didn't care about the Russians. I'm sure he would've just as soon let us storm this place and kill as many 'bad guys' as we could in order to get that drone away from them. But it's like I told him before: that's not how we operate. If Phantom Cell *does* operate that way ... is that something you want to be a part of?"

"They might not all be like that," Brighton said without much conviction. "But even if they are, I'm not. Maybe I can change things for the better."

"If anyone could, it'd be you," Cross agreed. "In any case, I can't make this decision for you, and it's not one you should be in any hurry to make for yourself. Give yourself time to think through all the possibilities. Just make sure you do what's best for you."

"All right, Commander," Brighton said, frowning in thought. "I'll let you know what I decide to do."

As Brighton walked away, Cross put his back to Lost Aspen and looked up at the sky. The phantom

sun's light shone dull and weak, casting a gloomy pall over everything. The South Pole's summer was almost over, and the cold winds hinted at a long winter still to come.

A shiver went up his spine – one that had nothing to do with the Antarctic cold.

MISSION DEBRIEFING

OPERATION

PHANTOM SUN 5678

PRIMARY OBJECTIVE

x Locate & secure crashed aircraft

- Maintain anonymity

SECONDARY OBJECTIVES

- Avoid hostilities with Russian forces

STATUS

2/3 COMPLETE

3245.98 ● ● ●

CROSS, RYAN

RANK: Lt. Commander
BRANCH: Navy Seal
PSYCH PROFILE: Team leader
of Shadow Squadron. Control
oriented and loyal, Cross insisted
on hand-picking each member of
his squad.

Our primary objective was to secure the crashed aircraft, but I refuse to believe that any piece of technology is worth risking forty-plus American lives, let alone waging war with Russian Special Forces. To my mind, we came away from this mission losing nothing except, possibly, a Combat Controller.

I have to admit that the thought of losing Brighton is unnerving. It would be hard -- maybe impossible -- to find a better man for the job...

Lieutenant Commander Ryan Cross

2019.681

CREATOR BIO(S)

AUTHOR

CARL BOWEN

Carl Bowen is a father, husband, and writer living in Lawrenceville, Georgia. He was born in Louisiana, lived briefly in England, and was raised in Georgia where he went to school. He has published a handful of novels, short stories, and comics. For Stone Arch Books, he has retold *20,000 Leagues Under the Sea*, *The Strange Case of Dr. Jekyll and Mr. Hyde*, *The Jungle Book*, *Aladdin and the Magic Lamp*, *Julius Caesar*, and *The Murders in the Rue Morgue*. He is the original author of *BMX Breakthrough* as well as the Shadow Squadron series.

INTEL

DECRYPTING

LOADING...

ARTIST

WILSON TORTOSA

Wilson "Wunan" Tortosa is a Filipino comic book artist best known for his works on *Tomb Raider* and the American relaunch of *Battle of The Planets* for Top Cow Productions. Wilson attended Philippine Cultural High School, then went on to the University of Santo Tomas where he graduated with a Bachelor's Degree in Fine Arts, majoring in Advertising.

ARTIST

BENNY FUENTES

Benny Fuentes lives in Villahermosa, Tabasco in Mexico, where the temperature is just as hot as the sauce. He studied graphic design in college, but now he works as a full-time illustrator in the comic book and graphic novel industry for companies like Marvel, DC Comics, and Top Cow Productions. He shares his home with two crazy cats, Chelo and Kitty, who act like they own the place.

2019.681

AUTHOR DEBRIEFING

ACCESS GRANTED

CARL BOWEN

Q/When and why did you decide to become a writer?

A/I've enjoyed writing ever since I was in school. I wrote as much as I could, hoping to become the next Lloyd Alexander or Stephen King, but I didn't sell my first story until I was in college. It had been a long wait, but the day I saw my story in print was one of the best days of my life.

Q/What made you decide to write *Shadow Squadron*?

A/As a kid, my heroes were always brave knights or noble loners who fought because it was their duty, not for fame or glory. I think the special ops soldiers of the US military embody those ideals. Their jobs are difficult and often thankless, so I wanted to show how cool their jobs are and also express my gratitude for our brave warriors.

Q/What inspires you to write?

A/My biggest inspiration is my family. My wife's love and support lifts me up when this job seems too hard to keep going. My son is another big inspiration.

He's three years old, and I want him to read my books and feel the same way I did when I read my favourite books as a kid. And if he happens to grow up to become an elite soldier in the US military, that would be pretty awesome, too.

Q/Describe what it was like to write these books.

A/The only military experience I have is a year I spent in the Army ROTC. It gave me a great respect for the military and its soldiers, but I quickly realized I would have made a pretty awful soldier. I recently got to test out a friend's arsenal of firearms, including a combat shotgun, an AR-15 rifle, and a Barrett M82 sniper rifle. We got to blow apart an old fax machine.

Q/What is your favourite book, movie, and game?

A/My favourite book of all time is *Don Quixote*. It's crazy and it makes me laugh. My favourite movie is either *Casablanca* or *Double Indemnity*, old black-and-white movies made before I was born. My favourite game, hands down, is *Skyrim*, in which you play a heroic dragon-slayer. But not even *Skyrim* can keep me from writing more *Shadow Squadron* stories, so you won't have to wait long to read more about Ryan Cross and his team. That's a promise.

INTEL

DECRYPTING

5678

COM CHATTER

-MISSION PREVIEW: Syrian rebels are in possession of a White Needle, or stolen chemical weapon, and plan to use it on an unknown target. Only Shadow Squadron has the talent and technology to locate and neutralize the missile before it's launched...

3245.98 ● ● ●

SHADOW SQUADRON

WHITE NEEDLE

CARL BOWEN

WHITE NEEDLE

Cross double-tapped his acknowledgement and led Williams around the back. No lights were on inside and no sounds came from within. Motioning Williams to take a position by the back door, Cross paused at the threshold. He gave three quick knocks.

NOK! NOK! NOK!

A moment later, a voice spoke from inside. "Jingle bells."

Cross gave a little smirk. "Batman smells," he answered, giving the agreed-upon password. Williams rolled his eyes.

"Wait," the inside voice said.

Cross heard a rattling of a makeshift barricade from inside. Then the door opened. A young Israeli in black fatigues held a sawed-off shotgun pointed at gut level. He looked Cross and Williams over with obvious confusion, noticing the lack of any identifying marks on their uniforms. "You're the Americans. Are you CIA?"

"Nope," Cross said. "Do you have some intel for us?"

"Inside," the Israeli said, backing off and lowering his shotgun. He disappeared into the house, prompting Cross and Williams to follow him. Williams closed the door behind them.

"I'm glad you made it," the Israeli soldier said. "Which one of you is the medic?"

"I am," Williams answered before Cross could stop him.

"Our orders didn't mention anything about a medic," Cross said. It was sheer chance that he'd picked Williams to accompany him to the house.

The Israeli sighed. "So this isn't a rescue?" he

asked. He paused at the threshold of an interior room. "I should've known."

"What's your name? Are you hurt?" Williams asked. "Do you need a medic?"

"My name is Benjamin," the man said, "and I'm fine. It's Asher who's injured. He's been shot." He headed into a nearby room.

Williams pushed past Cross and hurried into the next room with the Israeli. On a cot lay a second Israeli, who'd been stripped to the waist and heavily bandaged around his stomach with cut-up bedsheets. Williams knelt at the man's bedside and slung off his pack. The first Israeli leaned against the wall and looked down at his wounded comrade with tired worry.

"Hey, Asher, can you hear me?" Williams asked. He lay one palm over the wounded man's forehead and took his pulse at the wrist with his other hand. The man lay unconscious. Sweat gleamed on his skin, and a dark bruise peeked above the topmost edge of the bandage. "He's burning up." He looked up at the first Israeli. "Where was he hit, Benjamin?"

"In his back," Benjamin said. "On the right."

"Commander, please give me a hand," Williams said.

Cross knelt beside Williams. Together they levered Asher onto his left side. At Williams' nod, Cross cut away the bandage until only a thick square of gauze remained over the wound site. Deep, purple-red bruises covered most of the wounded man's lower back.

"Hold that there," Williams said. "No exit wound. Severe bruising. Non-responsive. How long ago did this happen?"

Benjamin took a moment to realize Williams was speaking to him. "Huh? Oh, yesterday. What time is it?" He checked his watch. "Maybe 24 hours ago. A little longer."

Williams winced. "That's not good," he said. He dug through his medical pack and produced a set of fresh bandages.

"What happened?" Cross asked.

"Stupid, blind carelessness," Benjamin said. "We

were in the mountains in Salma, monitoring a rebel cell. They were celebrating a victory and we were backing off to exfiltrate. We didn't realize they'd called up reinforcements to replace losses they'd taken. We blundered right into them, and they cut my team down. Asher and I got out and played *machboim* with them for a while until we found this place. They didn't seem too eager to follow us in here."

"*Machboim?*" Cross said.

"Hide and seek," Benjamin explained. "Anyway, when we got here I cleaned the wound and patched him up. I didn't think it was that bad at first. He just had a little bruising around the hole and very little bleeding. I thought we could wait for a rescue, but he's been getting worse all day."

"That's because he's bleeding internally," Williams said. He pressed stiff fingers hard into Asher's abdomen on the right side. The bruised flesh barely gave in at all. "See how rigid that is? His whole abdominal cavity is filling up with blood. He's got a high fever, which means he's got a severe infection.

His pulse is weak and he's barely breathing. He's not reacting when I poke him like this. It should hurt like crazy, but he's not even twitching."

"Can you take the bullet out?" Benjamin asked, trying to stay calm. "Will that help?"

"Judging from where it went in," Williams said, "it's probably at least nicked his liver, his spleen, or his kidney. For all I know it's sitting inside one of those organs like a cork. It's a miracle he's lasted as long as he has."

"Is there anything you can do?" Benjamin asked. "Anything at all?"

Williams put on his most calm, blank, professional expression. Cross had seen it before in the field – the day Second Lieutenant Neil Larssen had been killed in action during a covert op on an oil platform in the Gulf of Mexico.

"I'm sorry," Williams said. "It would've been unlikely even if you could've got him straight to a hospital."

Benjamin's face darkened. "His sisters will be devastated."

Cross backed off to give the Israeli a moment to feel his grief. He quietly tapped his canalphone. "High Road, this is Low Road," Cross said. "We need a pick-up for two friendlies, one injured."

Benjamin stood. "Where will you take us?" he asked Cross.

"Home," Cross said, "with a brief stopover at our base. We'll do everything we can for your man, I promise you that. But you'll owe us some information for the extraction."

"I'll tell you whatever you want to know," Benjamin said. He watched Williams finish re-bandaging his comrade's wounds.

When Williams was finished, he walked over to Cross and stood beside him. "He's not going to make it," he said, barely above a whisper.

2012.101